SOPHIE SHYOSAURUS

D0178453

Published in 2015 by Wayland

Text copyright © Brian Moses
Illustrations copyright © Mike Gordon

Wayland
338 Euston Road
London NW1 3BH

Wayland Australia
Level 17/207 Kent Street
Sydney, NSW 2000

All rights reserved

Senior editor: Victoria Brooker
Creative design: Basement68
Digital colour: Molly Hahn

British Library Cataloguing
in Publication Data:

Moses, Brian, 1950-
 Sophie Shyosaurus. --
   (Dinosaurs have feelings, too)
  1. Children's stories--Pictorial
   works.
  I. Title II. Series III. Gordon, Mike,
   1948 Mar. 16-
   823.9'2-dc23
ISBN: 978 0 7502 8087 7

Printed in China

Wayland is a division of
Hachette Children's Books,
an Hachette UK company.
www.hachette.co.uk

SOPHIE SHYOSAURUS

Written by
Brian Moses

Illustrated by
Mike Gordon

LONDON BOROUGH OF HACKNEY LIBRARIES	
HK12002481	
Bertrams	10/04/2015
	£6.99
	09/04/2015

WAYLAND

Can you see
Sophie Shyosaurus?

Sophie really is very shy and quite often, when visitors call, she hides away.

But maybe you can spot her?

Sophie doesn't like meeting adult dinosaurs. She blushes and gets tongue-tied.

She never knows what to say.

Sophie wants to go to parties, but she isn't happy being with dinosaurs she doesn't know.

She asks her Mum to stay with her until
she finds someone she can play with.

Sophie feels shy when she's asked
to talk in front of her class at school.
Her mouth goes dry and she
can't think of what to say.

Sometimes she starts to cry.

Sophie's Mum and Dad are always
telling her not to worry about it.

"It's OK to feel shy," her Dad tells her. "Everyone feels shy at sometime or other."

"When I first met the manager at Beastly Towers,
the hotel where I work," Sophie's Dad explained,
"I just didn't know what to say."

"And when I did say something, the words were wrong. That was all because I felt a bit shy."

"But I don't like feeling shy," Sophie said. "I love to dance, but if I know someone is watching, I feel embarrassed and I have to stop."

"Will I ever stop feeling shy?"
Sophie wondered.

"Let's see if we can help you," her Dad said. "When you meet other dinosaurs, there's no need to hide away. Let's practise what you might say."

Sometimes it helps to do something for someone, and to smile at them when you offer.

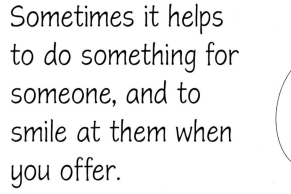

"Can I help you carry your bags?"

That someone you help may
even become a new friend.

Sometimes taking a special toy to
school can help when you're feeling shy.
You can cuddle your toy, or maybe someone
else will have the same toy and you
can play together.

Very soon other dinosaurs
may want to play with you as well.

"Everyone has something
they're good at,"
Sophie's Mum said.
"You're good at dancing."

"But if you feel shy when other dinosaurs are watching you, it's just because they like your dancing," her Dad said. "They might even join in too."

Sophie is still a little bit shy, but she's working hard every day at leaving her shyness behind.

And the other
day she even
won a medal
for her dancing.

NOTES FOR PARENTS AND TEACHERS

Read the book with children either individually or in groups.
Talk to them about what makes someone shy. How do
children feel when they are shy?

How would they picture that shyness? Would it feel like having
butterflies in your tummy, or being red faced, or wanting to be invisible?

Help children compose short poems about the times that they feel shy.
        I feel shy when I'm with children I haven't met before.
        I feel shy when I'm asked to talk in front of my class.
        I feel shy when everyone's watching me.
        I feel shy...

Talk to children about how they behave when they feel shy
and write down their ideas so they can be discussed.
        Days when I'm shy, I just want to hide.
        I want to be invisible, in a place where no one sees me.
        I want to be behind the settee, in another room,
        Just let me roll up into a ball
        and pretend I'm not here.

Remind them that shyness is a feeling, and like other feelings it can
come and go. Can they think of situations in which they don't feel
shy? Perhaps with friends and family, perhaps when they are
doing something they are good at.

Think about situations where children might feel shy and use them for role play. One child might play the part of an adult meeting a child for the first time. Help children write down what they might say on pieces of card and then practise saying the lines.

If a child has to give a talk at school, help them write out the talk first and practise saying it in front of the mirror. The more the lines are read aloud, the more confident children will get about saying them in front of others.

Can children find other words for 'shy' – timid, nervous, cautious, bashful. One of the dwarfs in the story of *Snow White* was called Bashful. Children might enjoy watching the film and looking out for him.

Always be positive when discussing shyness. Remind children that everyone is good at something and that confidence in this area can help children lose their shyness.

Explore the notion of shyness further through the sharing of picture books mentioned in the book list on page 32.

BOOKS TO SHARE

Little Miss Shy by Roger Hargreaves (Little Miss Classic Library)
Like most of the 'Mr Men' and 'Little Miss' books, this is a witty and engaging story that children will enjoy.

Two Shy Pandas by Julia Jarman (author)
& Susan Varley (illustrator) Published by Andersen 2012.
Panda and Pandora are two shy pandas who would love to speak to each other, but will they ever find the courage to do so?

I'm Shy (Your Feelings) by Karen Bryant-Mole (Wayland, 1999)
Through cartoons and humour this book aims to help young children understand their shyness.

Shaun the Shy Shark by Neil Griffiths & Peggy Collins
(Red Robin, 2008)
Shaun was so shy that the sight of
a jellyfish made him wobble!
Perfect for reading aloud.